STAR WARS REBELS

DROIDS IN DISTRESS

BASED ON THE *STAR WARS REBELS* EPISODES
"SPARK OF REBELLION," BY SIMON KINBERG,
"DROIDS IN DISTRESS," BY GREG WEISMAN, AND
"RISE OF THE OLD MASTERS," BY HENRY GILROY

WRITTEN BY MICHAEL KOGGE

DISNEP

LUCASFILM
PRESS

Los Angeles • New York

Printed in the United States of America

First Edition
1 3 5 7 9 10 8 6 4 2
G658-7729-4-14276
Library of Congress Control Number: 2014947311
ISBN 978-1-4847-0466-0

Visit the official *Star Wars* website: www.starwars.com

SUSTAINABLE FORESTRY INITIATIVE
Certified Chain of Custody
Promoting Sustainable Forestry
www.sfiprogram.org
SFI-01415
The SFI label applies to the text stock

PART 1
EZRA'S STORY

CHAPTER 1

Fourteen-year-old Ezra

Bridger's life changed the morning an Imperial Star Destroyer rumbled over his communications tower hideout. The massive vessel didn't shoot at him, nor did its complement of TIE fighters spot him on the tower's observation deck. Rather, it was Ezra who acted. He grabbed his backpack, got on his jump bike, and followed the craft to Capital City on Lothal. Wherever the Empire went, there was expensive tech Ezra could steal—and more helmets to add to his collection.

In the marketplace, Ezra found Commandant Aresko, the head of the local

Imperial Academy, and his second-in-command, Taskmaster Grint, picking on a Gotal fruit seller who didn't have a sales license. As white-armored stormtroopers began to drag the fruit seller away, Ezra walked past Aresko and unclipped the new-model comlink from the man's belt. Moving out of sight, Ezra put on his most adult voice and spoke into the comlink: "All officers to the main square. This is a code-red emergency!"

Ezra watched in glee as Aresko, Grint, and the stormtroopers released the fruit seller and rushed off to the square. The fruit seller thanked Ezra and gave him a few juicy jogans as a reward. Ezra then headed to the square himself, via the rooftops.

Perched on a roof's edge, he peered down into the square. Imperial Supply Master Lyste was supervising stormtroopers loading hover crates onto speeder bikes. Aresko and Grint arrived, huffing and puffing. They demanded to know why Lyste had called a code red. Lyste claimed he hadn't.

While the Imperials argued, Ezra noticed a human male with a goatee and a ponytail standing in the square. There was something strange about him, something that made Ezra tremble. The man tapped his thigh twice, signaling a muscular nonhuman and a female in multicolored Mandalorian armor who didn't look much older than Ezra.

The girl in armor walked past Lyste and the stormtroopers, flipping a round object at a speeder bike. The object magnetically clamped to the vehicle's side. Moments after she left, the bike exploded.

Those troopers who weren't blasted off their feet rushed about, searching for the culprit. But the girl was long gone.

"Get those crates out of here! Keep them secure at all costs," Lyste yelled.

A stormtrooper leapt onto the lead bike

and sped away—only to skid to a halt to avoid colliding with a landspeeder. Its driver was the man with the goatee. To Ezra's utter amazement, the man leapt out of the landspeeder, kicked the rider off the bike, then drew his blaster and fired at the oncoming stormtrooper squad. His burly nonhuman comrade thumped out from an alley to assist, hurling stormtroopers around as if they were rag dolls.

Below Ezra, the lead Imperial bike lay unattended—along with the two crates attached to it. Whatever was inside them must be highly valuable to have caused the confrontation. If he sold the contents, he might never have to pick pockets again.

Taking a deep breath, he jumped off the roof and landed in the bike's seat. "Thanks for doing the heavy lifting," he said to the man and his bruiser friend, then heeled the pedals and was off, zipping through the city.

All of a sudden, the girl in the Mandalorian armor dropped from the sky to land on Ezra's rearmost crate. She detached it from his bike and fell away with it. "If that big guy catches you, he'll end you," she said, her voice filtered through her helmet.

Ezra couldn't retrieve the crate, because the man and the bruiser trailed him on stolen bikes. He veered down alleys, snaked through an Imperial blockade, and got onto the freeway. The would-be thieves remained on his tail, now pursued by stormtroopers on bikes. The troopers fired at all of them—and Ezra's bike was hit.

Ezra lost control and his bike tumbled over the partition into the other lane. The man followed him, swinging his bike in front of Ezra's.

"I've got plans for that crate, so time to give it up. Today's not your day," the man said.

TIE fighters roared down from the sky. "Day's not over yet," Ezra said. TIE lasers struck the man's bike, and Ezra raced away, off the freeway into the grasslands.

The TIEs pursued, unleashing their cannons. Ezra zigzagged between the prairie mounds but could only evade the guns for so long. One finally scored a hit. Ezra pressed the cargo detachment button, then flew off the bike as it crashed.

A TIE swerved around to finish off Ezra. He stood there, waiting for the inevitable, when a diamond-shaped freighter burst out of the clouds and blasted the TIE into a fireball.

The man with the ponytail emerged from the freighter's cargo hatch. "Want a ride?"

Ezra turned to the hover crate. Having almost been vaporized because of it, he couldn't leave it there. He switched the crate's repulsors to max, then grabbed it and jumped.

The crate landed on the freighter's ramp. Ezra clawed up behind it.

CHAPTER 2

All of Ezra's efforts to save the crate had been meaningless. The freighter's crew decided to sell its contents—an assortment of blasters—to a horned Devaronian named Cikatro Vizago. Being one against five, Ezra was powerless to stop them.

Nonetheless, that didn't mean he couldn't take something of equivalent value. While they did their business in a refugee camp, Ezra snuck into the freighter they called the *Ghost*. Using the astromech arm he'd stashed in his backpack, he unlocked the door to a sleeping cabin.

Ezra's instinct for finding the most valuable item in a pocket led him to a drawer underneath the bunk. He took out an object with many sides, then a cylinder that looked like a glow rod. When he activated it, a blade of crackling blue energy extended from the lens.

"Hand me the lightsaber," said Kanan Jarrus, the man with the goatee. He stood in the doorway with Hera, the freighter's Twi'lek pilot, and the crew's crotchety astromech droid, Chopper. The droid must've been on the ship and ratted Ezra out.

Ezra waved the blade in the air. "Lightsaber? Isn't that the weapon of the Jedi?"

"Give it to me," Kanan said.

Ezra deactivated the blade and did as the man requested. But as he left the cabin, he clutched the other object he'd taken from the drawer.

He went into the galley, where the girl who wore the funky Mandalorian armor drank a glass of blue milk. She was the only one of their

crew whose name Ezra did not know—and the only one he'd really wanted to know. Ezra couldn't stop looking at her. She colored her hair like she colored her armor, with stripes of different colors.

"Who are you people?" he asked.

"We're a crew. A team. In some ways, a family," she said.

"What happened to your real family?"

"The Empire," she said. "What happened to yours?"

Ezra didn't answer that question. Those memories still hurt.

Zeb, the brawny Lasat who had tossed around the stormtroopers, came by and told the girl that Kanan had called a meeting in the common room.

"Sabine," the girl said to Ezra as she walked out. "My name's Sabine."

Now that Ezra knew her name, he wanted to know more. He climbed into the *Ghost*'s ventilation duct and crawled down into a supply closet in the common room, where Kanan spoke to the others: "Vizago acquired the flight plan for an Imperial transport ship full of Wookiees."

Ezra had heard of Wookiees. They were a strong, proud people whom the Empire had enslaved for their strength and engineering skills.

"I owe those hairy beasts," Zeb said. "They saved some of my people."

Shifting for a better position, Ezra clanked his elbow against the closet wall. He tried to climb back into the duct, but Kanan opened the closet and Ezra fell out.

"Can we please get rid of this Loth-rat?" Zeb growled. Chopper concurred with a beep.

Unexpectedly, Sabine spoke up. "No. We can't."

Hera joined her, saying the boy knew too much. She promised to keep an eye on Ezra.

CHAPTER 3

At first, the mission to rescue the Wookiees went as planned. The *Ghost* docked with the Imperial transport, under the pretense that Governor Tarkin had ordered them to transfer a Wookiee captive. Though Zeb failed miserably at playing the hairless Wookiee captive, he had a talent for bashing stormtroopers, so he, Kanan, Sabine, and Chopper easily boarded the transport.

That was when Ezra's fears about the mission came true. He and Hera had stayed behind in the *Ghost*'s cockpit, where they had a clear view of the Star Destroyer *Lawbringer* suddenly exiting hyperspace.

Hera tried to contact the others, but their comm was jammed. "Ezra, you need to board the transport and warn them."

"No, no way," he said. Survival on Lothal demanded he look out only for himself. "Why would I risk my life for a bunch of strangers?"

"If all you do is fight for your own life, then your life's worth nothing," she said. "They need you, Ezra."

Hera's words touched something inside Ezra. As much as he liked living alone, he missed his family. If the crew needed him, maybe it meant he could become part of their family.

Ezra went aboard the transport.

He found Kanan and Zeb about to blow open the brig where the Wookiees were imprisoned. "It's a trap," Ezra shouted. "Run!"

Sure enough, the brig's blast door opened, revealing stormtroopers behind it. The three fled down the corridor, only to be blocked by more stormtroopers and an Imperial officer.

Fortunately, Sabine and Chopper accomplished their part of the mission. The artificial gravity turned off, throwing the Imperials off balance. Ezra, Kanan, and Zeb flew past them. The microgravity lasted until they reached the docking bay, where Chopper and Sabine joined them. Kanan ordered everyone back through the air lock, into the *Ghost*.

The Imperial officer arrived in the docking bay with stormtroopers. He grabbed Ezra from behind, pulling him back from the others.

Zeb turned around in the air lock. There was little he could do with the stormtroopers firing shots. "Sorry, kid," he said, and the air lock slammed shut.

The stormtroopers tossed Ezra into a holding cell on the *Lawbringer*. He had sat there for hours, feeling stupid for listening to Hera, when the Imperial officer entered.

"I am Agent Kallus of the Imperial Security Bureau. And you are?"

"Jabba the Hutt," Ezra replied. He would never tell the Empire anything about himself. As for the crew of the *Ghost,* he'd rat them out if he could. "Look, I just met those guys today. I don't know anything."

"You're not here for what you know, 'Jabba.' You're here to be used as bait," Kallus said. He stared at Ezra for a moment, then walked out.

The stormtrooper guards came forward and shook Ezra's backpack, taking everything except the object from Kanan's cabin. Ezra sat on it before they could notice it, and after the troopers left, he examined it, sensing that something lay inside. But he couldn't figure out how to open it, so he tossed it at the cell door and closed his eyes.

"This is Master Obi-Wan Kenobi," a voice said. Ezra peeked at the object, which projected the hologram of a bearded man in robes.

"This message is a warning—and a reminder—for any surviving Jedi. Trust in the Force," the hologram said.

Old-timers on Lothal sometimes whispered stories of the Jedi, who had extraordinary powers and wielded lightsabers. But they were dead—weren't they? Could Kanan be one of them, in hiding?

Ezra would never know if he stayed in the cell. Remembering how the thieves had faked

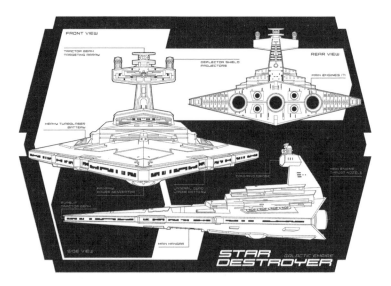

Governor Tarkin's orders, he went to the door. "You bucket heads will be sorry when my uncle the Emperor finds out you're keeping me," he said to the guards outside, and pretended to choke.

The stormtroopers entered the cell to check if their Imperial bait could breathe. Ezra, who had been hiding near the door, dashed out and locked it behind him.

He found his possessions in the storeroom, along with helmets. He put on one made for cadets. On its radio, he heard an Imperial officer say that the Wookiees were being transferred to the spice mines of Kessel. He also heard that "rebels" had infiltrated the lower hangar.

Had the crew of the *Ghost* come back for Ezra?

He wriggled into a ventilation duct and crawled toward the hangar. Peering through the duct grille, Ezra saw Kanan, Hera, Sabine, and Zeb. Somehow they had landed the *Ghost* inside the Star Destroyer's docking bay.

Ezra dropped down before them and promptly received Zeb's fist in his helmet. Ezra took off the helmet. "First you ditch me, then you hit me?"

"How was I supposed to know it was you? You were wearing a bucket!" Zeb said.

Blaster bolts from Kallus and his stormtroopers ended their argument. Ezra sprinted with the rebels back into the *Ghost*. They wouldn't have made it if not for the symbol of the starbird Sabine had sprayed on the floor. Its thermal paint detonated, tearing a hole in the docking bay and sucking stormtroopers into outer space.

Once the *Ghost* had made the jump to lightspeed, Ezra told the crew what he had heard on the helmet radio. "I know where they're taking the Wookiees. The spice mines of Kessel."

This stunned them. Kessel was the Empire's most dreaded slave labor camp. No one who was sent there ever returned.

Hera plotted the course. They couldn't let the Wookiees endure such a punishment.

CHAPTER 4

Ezra had never been to another planet before, but if Kessel was any indication of what the rest of the galaxy looked like, he had no problem spending his life on Lothal. Kessel was a shrine to pollution. Huge mining columns dotted the world, gushing out toxic waste that smogged the skies and spoiled the surface.

The *Ghost* slipped past orbital security to descend toward a mining platform. Ezra, Sabine, and Kanan leapt out and were greeted by stormtrooper blaster fire. Ezra knocked out a few stormtroopers with his slingshot and rushed toward the Wookiee prisoners the stormtroopers escorted.

While the others kept the troopers busy, he unlocked the Wookiees' binders with his astromech arm. The Wookiees roared in gratitude and joined the fight. All was going well until Imperial reinforcements arrived. TIE fighters forced the *Ghost* to fly away, and an Imperial transport unloaded even more stormtroopers. None other than Agent Kallus led them.

Kanan strode into the field of battle, holstering his blaster and igniting his lightsaber. Both sides paused in wonder at his blue blade, until Kallus broke the silence: "Focus your fire on . . . the Jedi!"

Ezra blinked, not believing what he saw. With only his lightsaber, Kanan deflected bolts back at the shooters, taking on the platoon by himself. "Get the Wookiees out of here!" he shouted.

Zeb and Sabine herded the Wookiees into

an empty shipping container the *Ghost* could retrieve when it swooped around. The Wookiee leader, a giant silverback whom Ezra had learned was called Wullffwarro, howled and tried to go the other way. A blaster bolt in the shoulder grounded him, and Ezra and Zeb came to his aid. Then Ezra saw what had enraged him.

A stormtrooper chased a Wookiee cub on a catwalk that bridged two platforms. The cub must be Kitwarr, Wullffwarro's son.

Defying Zeb's cry for him to stay, Ezra ran after them.

The stormtrooper spun and aimed his blaster at Ezra. Like he had on Lothal, Ezra jumped. His strength came from more than just the muscles in his legs; it was as if his heart and mind boosted him over the stormtrooper. He landed on the catwalk and fired his slingshot. A stun-ball hit the trooper and caused him to fall off the catwalk.

Ezra scooped up Kitwarr. He couldn't see the *Ghost* anywhere in the sky. All he saw was

Agent Kallus marching down the catwalk,
blaster raised.

"It's over for you, Jedi. Master and
apprentice, such a rare find these days. Perhaps
you are the only two left."

"I don't know where you get your delusions,
bucket head," Ezra said. "I work alone."

"Not this time," said a familiar voice.

Kanan stood on the *Ghost* as it rose from under the catwalk. Wielding his lightsaber, he deflected Kallus's blaster shots back at the man.

Kallus tumbled over the catwalk, saving himself from oblivion only by catching a support beam far below.

After ferrying the Wookiees to a friendly gunship, the rebels returned to Lothal to drop off Ezra at his communications tower. But Ezra didn't want to leave without a memento. He bumped into Kanan, unclipped the lightsaber off the man's belt, and kept it hidden until he had disembarked.

The tower looked just as Ezra had left it, with dust collecting on the helmets and tech he'd accumulated over the years. Yet they all felt rather old now, as if they were possessions from another life.

"You can keep the lightsaber you stole and

let it become just another dusty souvenir," Kanan said, coming up behind Ezra. "Or you can give it back and come with us, to learn the ways of the Force and what it truly means to be a Jedi."

"I thought the Empire wiped out all the Jedi," Ezra said.

"Not all of us," Kanan said.

Ezra couldn't hide in his tower anymore— not after seeing what the galaxy had to offer. He returned to his new family on the *Ghost*. His life had changed.

PART 2
DISRUPTED

CHAPTER 5

Ezra entered Lothal's main spaceport, with Chopper rolling beside him. He used to go there frequently, dipping his hand into pockets and purses. Now he was going to use the same talents on a much larger scale. Low on supplies and fuel, the crew of the *Ghost* had no choice but to accept Cikatro Vizago's job to steal a cargo shipment from an Imperial minister.

"Boarding Star-Commuter Shuttle ST-45, bound for Garel," the dispatcher said over the intercom. This was Ezra's cue. Pretending not to recognize Sabine and Zeb in the passenger line, Ezra and Chopper cut in front of them and entered the shuttle.

"How rude," Zeb said.

Ezra and Chopper lingered along the side of the shuttle's forward section to let the other passengers shuffle past. Two who boarded behind Sabine and Zeb fit Vizago's descriptions of the marks. The human female was Maketh Tua, an Imperial minister, and her companion was Amda Wabo, a round-eyed, tusked Aqualish trader.

Tua checked her boarding pass. "This way, Mister Wabo. We have seats in the front."

The Aqualish responded in his native language, which sounded like nerf bleats. Tua looked around the ship. "Where is that translator?"

"Coming, Minister!" said an aristocratic voice. "Come along, Artoo."

Ezra saw not a prince, but a protocol droid plated in gold and a blue-domed R2 unit. The protocol droid, identifying himself as C-3PO

and his counterpart as R2-D2, translated for
Tua and led Wabo to the front.

Kanan slipped into the shuttle as the hatch
was about to close. He sat next to Ezra and
Chopper, though Ezra pretended not to know
who he was.

The shuttle launched and jumped to
hyperspace. Kanan tapped his thigh, signaling
Ezra to do his part. Ezra started to push
Chopper. "Will you cut it out? You have plenty
of room!"

The passengers turned around in their
seats. Chopper fought back by extending his
electroshock prod and zapping Ezra.

"Isn't there some rule against droids in the
passenger area?" Kanan called to the RX-24
droid pilot.

RX-24 rotated his blinking head to address
Ezra. "Sir, your astromech must proceed to the
back of the craft."

Ezra acted outraged and pointed at C-3PO
and R2-D2. "If my astromech's banished, then

those two astromechs should be banished, too."

"Astromech? *Me?*" C-3PO said. "I have never been so insulted! I'll have you know that I am a protocol droid, fluent in six million forms of—"

CHOPPER

"Pilot," Tua cut in, "these two droids are with me on *Imperial* business."

"Sorry, ma'am, but these are *Imperial* regulations," RX-24 said.

With a clunking sigh, C-3PO joined R2-D2 and followed Chopper to the rear of the shuttle's forward section. Ezra sat back in his seat. Kanan winked for a job well done.

Without C-3PO, the misunderstandings mounted between Tua and Wabo. Zeb leaned over to them. "Excuse me, but if it's of any help, my ward here is quite fluent in Aqualish."

Seated next to Zeb, Sabine waved off his comment. "I would never presume, though it would be good practice for my level-five exams at the Imperial Academy."

Tua warmed to her. "You're a level-five Academy student? I was, too, once upon a time."

Ezra found it hard to hear the rest of their conversation over C-3PO's constant chatter in the back. The protocol droid complained to his counterpart that their mission for Lothal's Governor Pryce was in danger of failure. Chopper shut him up with a sharp beep.

"Ask Mr. Wabo where the shipment is being held," Ezra heard Tua say to Sabine.

Sabine translated Wabo's response as "Bay Seventeen." Her grin told Ezra she had kept the real number for herself.

CHAPTER 6

The shuttle landed at the Garel spaceport. Tua and Wabo left with the two droids, and Ezra followed them out. A contingent of stormtroopers stood outside. "Take us to Bay Seventeen," Tua ordered. The troopers escorted her party away.

Ezra waited by a stack of cargo crates near the terminal. Chopper rolled past, followed by Zeb and Sabine, who whispered, "Bay Seven."

Ezra stepped behind the crates and climbed the stack. He found the ventilation duct for the terminal building, jimmied free the cover, and crawled inside. Grime coated his clothes and hands as he wormed down the duct.

"This is disgusting," he said into his comlink. "Kanan, I thought you were going to teach me Jedi stuff. So far, all I'm doing is thieving—which I already know how to do!"

"Not my first choice, either," Kanan commed back. "But the *Ghost* needs fuel and food."

The duct turned vertical, forcing Ezra to shinny up it. He elbowed open the vent cover at the top of the shaft and emerged on a hangar rooftop. Wiping his dirty hands on his dirty pants, he gave himself a running start and long-jumped from roof to roof. When he reached the seventh rooftop, he found the duct and dropped through it to land in Bay Seven.

Shipping crates filled the hangar but Ezra didn't look to see what was inside. He went to the bay control panel, took out his astromech arm, and used it to override the lock. The huge bay doors opened, revealing Kanan, Zeb, and Sabine in the corridor outside. Zeb's bo-rifle was slung over his back, and Sabine wore her

REBEL
GHOST

Mandalorian armor and helmet. They stepped
into the hangar, while Kanan stayed back to
type a code into Bay Eight's control panel.

"Well, kid, you pulled it off," Zeb said.

"Was there any doubt?" Ezra asked.

"Yes," Zeb and Sabine said in unison.

A few weeks earlier, Ezra would have

frowned and walked away. Now he realized this was their dry sense of humor. Still, he wasn't ready to laugh at himself—not yet.

Hera's voice came over his comlink. "Do we know what Vizago has us stealing?"

"Go see, Zeb," Kanan answered, entering the hangar. Bay Eight's doors opened in the corridor behind him. The *Ghost* was coming in to land.

Zeb pried loose a crate lid, then cursed, appalled by what he saw inside. Sabine removed what looked like a blaster yet was fatter than a DH-17 pistol. A gas cartridge the size of three ammo packs made up the bulk.

"Whoa—they're T-7 Ion Disruptors," Sabine said. "These were banned by the Senate. You can short-circuit an entire ship with these."

Zeb glowered. "That's not why they were banned."

"Get them aboard before company comes," Kanan said.

Ezra got to work, switching on the anti-grav

controls for each crate, while the others pushed them into the corridor. Zeb remained sullen and didn't put much effort into moving crates.

Chopper, meanwhile, had found a good spot to keep a photoreceptor and auditory sensor trained on Hangar Bay Seventeen. Minister Tua, the two droids, Wabo, and their stormtrooper escort looked around the empty bay.

"I don't understand. Where are the Emperor's disruptors?" Tua asked.

The R2 unit beeped in alarm. "Yes," his protocol counterpart assured him. "She said disruptors. Now shush."

Chopper recognized the astromech's response as typical of the new R2 series. Compassion was the biggest flaw in their programming.

Wabo pointed at markings on the wall and hollered in his language. The 3PO unit translated. "Apparently, the cargo is in Bay

Seven, so Amda Wabo wonders why we are here."

Tua frowned. "The girl told me seventeen."

"In Aqualish, a translator can easily confuse seven with seventeen," the 3PO unit said.

"To Bay Seven—double time!" Tua said.

Chopper radioed Hera to ready the *Ghost*. The Imperials were coming.

Zeb knew the damage disruptors could do—and why the Imps should never get their hands on them. So when he saw the stormtroopers rushing down the corridor, he felt relief that there was an outlet for his rage.

Leaving the last crates for Ezra to push, Zeb approached the Imps. "There a problem here?"

The stormtroopers lifted their blasters. Tua, Wabo, and the droids came up behind them. "Amda Wabo says those crates contain his disruptors," said C-3PO.

FREEDOM FIGHTER
CHOPPER

"Must be some mistake," Zeb said. "Can't possibly be disruptors in there, 'cause they're illegal, right?"

"That's irrelevant. We're going to search your crates," Tua said.

"Be my guest," Zeb said.

The stormtrooper commander waved two

troopers forward. Zeb let them pass, then grinned. "On second thought . . ."

Zeb pulled his bo-rifle off his shoulder and spun, bashing the two stormtroopers from behind. Then he whirled and slammed his huge frame into the commander.

He didn't wait for the bodies to hit the ground. He activated his rifle into shock-staff mode and charged the other stormtroopers. "You want disruption, I'll give you disruption!"

He punched with one fist while electrocuting troopers with his staff. In such close quarters, the stormtroopers couldn't get off shots without potentially hitting each other.

Ezra helped out, firing his slingshot. Kanan hurried into the corridor and picked off troopers with his blaster. "Get those crates on the *Ghost*—now!" Kanan yelled to Ezra.

Zeb hoped the boy would take his time. Smashing stormtroopers was too much fun to stop so soon.

• • •

Chopper wheeled past the stormtroopers, who were too busy being pummeled by Zeb to notice him. He veered into Hangar Bay Eight and rolled up the *Ghost*'s ramp into the cargo hold, where Sabine and Ezra unloaded crates.

"Oh, look. Chopper made friends," Sabine said.

Chopper rotated his dome to find the 3PO and R2 units ascending the ramp behind him.

"I told you that old C1 knew what he was doing. We're safe in here," the 3PO unit said.

A circuit in Chopper's motivator blew, causing his arm to smack against his dome. Of course he knew what he was doing. As for being "old," he was only a few decades past his manufacturer's expiry date. The universe was full of clunkers more antiquated than him.

The R2 unit took his counterpart's insult a step further, identifying Chopper and the crew as thieves. "Thieves? Here? That's ridiculous!" said the protocol droid.

Kanan and Zeb ran up the ramp. "Spectre-1

to *Ghost,* we're good to go!" Kanan said. "Spectre-5, let's get restraining bolts on these Imperial droids."

"On it," Sabine said.

Chopper chortled when he saw what only a droid could recognize—sheer horror in the 3PO unit's photoreceptors at the mention of restraining bolts.

CHAPTER 7

Nightmares haunted Zeb. Unable to sleep during the trip through hyperspace, he wandered the *Ghost*. But pacing the corridors didn't purge his nightmares, because the nightmares were more than dreams—they were real. They were his memories of seeing fellow Lasat being disintegrated atom by atom as they endured a slow death by disruptor beam.

He found Kanan in the main corridor. "Kanan, a word?"

"Can it wait?" Kanan asked. "If I don't confirm our rendezvous with Vizago, we'll have done all this for nothing. We might not have the fuel to fly again."

"Yeah, about that . . . Maybe this time we don't sell to Vizago," Zeb said. "Maybe we get those disruptors outta circulation instead."

Still wearing her helmet, Sabine emerged from her cabin holding restraining bolts. "Least we got them out of *Imperial* circulation," she said. "When I was translating, I found out they were shipping those T-7s as prototypes, so the Empire could mass-produce them on Lothal."

"See, Zeb? Perfect crime," Kanan said. "We steal weapons meant for the Empire and sell them for credits we desperately need to keep this bird flying."

He squeezed Zeb's shoulder and walked down the corridor. Sabine headed toward the cargo hold, calling back, "Hey, if we need more credits, maybe Vizago will buy the two droids."

"Good idea," Kanan said.

Zeb's head sunk and he went back into his cabin. The nightmares continued.

Rations weren't the only thing Ezra had to share with Zeb. They also shared cabins—or were supposed to. On that trip, Zeb was in a particularly foul mood and shut the cabin door in Ezra's face. And no amount of banging would convince Zeb to open it.

Hera called Ezra to join her in the cockpit. He did, in a foul mood now himself.

"Maybe you can cut Zeb a little slack today," Hera said. "Do you know what a T-7 disruptor is? What it does to an organic being?"

"Uh, no . . ." Ezra said.

"Well, Zeb knows. Because it's what the Imperials used on his people when they cleared his homeworld. Very few Lasat survived. And none remain on Lasan."

"I . . . I guess I could cut him a little slack," Ezra said. No one had told him that Zeb was one of the last of his people. He thought the big lugs lived all over the galaxy, like Rodians and Ugnaughts and red-eyed Duros. And he knew the Empire could be cruel and severe, but to virtually exterminate an entire species? That was . . . *evil.*

"Good man," Hera said. "So, how's the Jedi training going with Kanan?"

"Jedi training? Never heard of it," Ezra said.

Hera's head-tails twitched. "Really? We'll see about that."

The navicomputer chimed and the starlines shifted. Through the canopy loomed the blue-green orb of Ezra's home planet once again.

C-3PO's protocol processor halted him from apologizing, but it seemed that R2-D2 had been correct. The freighter's crew were thieves, and he and R2 were stolen merchandise to be sold.

R2 tried to tell the thieves that they were on loan to the Empire and that their true

master would pay well for their return. The girl in Mandalorian gear and the Lasat listened, but their leader did not seem persuaded.

There was no use in attempting to run. Restraining bolts restricted them from any movement the crew didn't desire. But there was a slight chance—845 to 1—that C-3PO might be able to do something to increase the odds of their being rescued.

When the freighter landed and the thieves began off-loading crates, C-3PO excused himself from the cargo bay so as not to be in their way. He went into the cockpit and sent a coded message to the woman they were on loan to, Governor Arihnda Pryce.

"This is C-3PO, human-cyborg relations. My counterpart and I were abducted from the spaceport on Garel by criminals, thieves, *outlaws.*"

"Have no fear," responded a male voice. Though it obviously wasn't Governor Pryce's,

C-3PO had been instructed to trust whomever answered the call. "Help is on the way."

C-3PO would have preferred to know what kind of help and how much it would move the odds in his favor.

Kanan didn't care much for Cikatro Vizago. The Devaronian had his horns deep in the galaxy's criminal underworld. But as Hera had insisted time and again, who else could fund their fight against the Empire?

The Devaronian picked up a disruptor from the crates the *Ghost*'s crew had brought into the clearing on Lothal. His black fingernails clicked against the disruptor's gas cartridges. "I can make some beautiful music with this."

"They're not that kind of instrument," Zeb snarled.

"You just have to know how to play them," Vizago said, "and how to play those who want to buy them."

Zeb appealed to Kanan with the most desperate of looks. He didn't want to sell the disruptors to Vizago. But they didn't have a choice. They needed the credits. And Vizago's IG-RM droids had already begun loading the crates onto two speeders.

"Let's get this over with," Kanan mumbled.

Vizago peered through the disruptor's scope. "What's this? You were followed?"

"That's not possible," Hera said.

Possible or not, the Empire was there. In the distance, Kanan saw an Imperial freighter carrying two AT-DP walkers zooming toward them.

Vizago waved to his war droids. "Leave the rest of the crates. We're gone."

Kanan grabbed Vizago's arm. "You haven't paid us."

Vizago wrested his arm free from Kanan's grip. "Cikatro Vizago doesn't pay for half the shipment, and he doesn't pay for trouble with Imperials."

The Devaronian hopped into a speeder. "My friends, I hope you live to bargain another day," he said. The speeders tore off into the grasslands.

The Imperial freighter neared, ignoring Vizago's fleeing speeders. Kanan could guess who was behind the attack if the *Ghost*'s crew was their priority—Agent Kallus.

Since they weren't getting paid, a new objective became clear. Kanan gave Zeb a knowing look. "We can't let these disruptors fall into Imperial hands."

R2-D2 started rolling toward an open crate, C-3PO in tow. "What are you doing?" C-3PO asked.

The droid tinkered with a disruptor in the crate, and the disruptor began to whine. Kanan realized what the droid was doing—as did Sabine.

"Of course! Overload the disruptors and— *boom!*" she said. "Good call, little guy."

The little astromech might've just saved

their lives. Kanan looked at the others. "Hera, help Sabine open the crates. Zeb, Ezra, line 'em up. We'll use the crates for cover until they're ready to blow."

The crew went to work as the oncoming freighter dropped the two AT-DP walkers from its undercarriage. They landed with a thunk and opened fire. Kanan took a disruptor from a crate, aimed at a walker, and pulled the trigger.

The T-7 prototype worked as designed. The disruptor's beam struck the AT-DP's hull, which sparkled with ionized energy before it toppled and crashed.

Before Kanan could shoot at the other walker, its lasers pounded the ground near him. He flew off his feet, losing the disruptor.

Kanan landed with a smack, then lifted his head to see a blurry Hera sprinting toward the second walker. He almost yelled for her to run away, but she wouldn't have listened. She shot at the walker's head with her blaster pistol, causing it to turn away from Kanan.

Zeb rushed to him and picked him up from the ground. Kanan's vision had improved, and now he saw Hera weaving between the stone circle, leading the walker on a wild nerf chase.

He also saw the enemy freighter land. Stormtroopers were disgorged from its bay, led by the Imperial officer Kanan had suspected.

"Advance and fire," Agent Kallus told his troopers.

CHAPTER 8

Kallus almost chuckled. The
protocol droid who'd sent him the message
shambled out to thank the Imperials—then
hurried back when the stormtroopers returned
his gratitude with gunfire.

Idiotic machine, thought Kallus. He hadn't
brought a platoon to rescue droids. He was here
to catch rebels, who hid behind crates like the
cowards they were. Since they refused to show
themselves, he would draw them out, starting
with the oversized alien who should have been
eliminated a long time ago.

Kallus unslung a weapon he'd taken as a

trophy on a past assignment. "You! Lasat!" he called. "Face me."

The alien turned, eyes widening when he saw the weapon Kallus flaunted. He leapt over the crates and charged, extending his bo-rifle into a staff.

"Only the Honor Guard of Lasan may carry a bo-rifle," the Lasat snarled.

"I know. I removed it from a guardsman myself," Kallus said. He extended his bo-rifle in similar fashion, and their staffs met in a loud thwack.

The alien wielded his staff with incredible strength and pushed Kallus backward. But if Kallus could incite the alien into a mindless rage, he could force him to make a fatal mistake.

"I was there when Lasan fell. I know why you fear those disruptors," Kallus said. "I gave the order to use them."

The Lasat howled and his swings became wilder. Kallus jumped, ducked, and slipped in a jab. Electricity crackled all around the alien's body, and he staggered back.

As much as he wanted to, Kallus couldn't finish the Lasat off just yet. The rebels had shoved hover crates beneath the AT-DP walker and the advancing stormtroopers, and they suddenly exploded. The walker wobbled and collapsed, while stormtroopers went soaring into the air. Kallus and the Lasat both barely managed to stay on their feet. Yet the Lasat had suffered electrocution, which made his disorientation worse.

Kallus struck again with his staff. The Lasat dropped to his knees, quivering from the shock. "Demonstration complete," Kallus said.

He shifted his staff into its rifle mode. Not only would he soon catch the last of the Jedi; he would also eliminate the last of the Lasat.

"No!" cried Ezra, seeing Kallus take aim at Zeb.

It couldn't end like that. Not after all Ezra and Zeb had been through. Not after all their arguments and dustups. Not after Ezra had learned the sad fate of Zeb's people.

Zeb, despite his hot temper, his unbearable odor, and his constant teasing, was Ezra's friend—a friend Ezra didn't want to lose.

Before he knew what he was doing, Ezra reached out, and through his fingers he felt a pulse, a power—a Force. It threw Kallus backward, away from Zeb.

Ezra stood there, stunned. Had he just done that?

Zeb remained on his knees, still twitching from the electrical shock, still alive.

After everyone had gotten aboard the *Ghost* and it was safe in hyperspace, Kanan and the crew gathered around Zeb. The Lasat lay on the cargo bay floor, recovering. Kanan helped Zeb to his feet.

"Thanks, mate. Appreciate the save," Zeb said.

"Wasn't me. It was Ezra," Kanan said.

Zeb stared at Ezra in surprise. The boy appeared equally surprised, perhaps unsettled by what he had done. Kanan no longer had any doubts about teaching the kid. He had listened to what Hera had said to him, and he had seen what the boy had done. This time, instead of saving himself, Ezra had saved a friend.

"Ezra," Kanan said. "Your formal training starts tomorrow."

Near the air lock on his blockade runner, Senator Bail Organa of Alderaan met the leader of the thieves who had stolen his droids. Except they weren't thieves. Thieves would have held C-3PO and R2-D2 for ransom. The tall man who brought the droids aboard asked for nothing in return.

Bail still gave him credits. That group could use the money. A sensor scan of their freighter showed that it was low on fuel.

"That's very generous," said the man.

"I'm very fond of these two droids." Bail patted R2-D2's dome. "The simplest gesture of kindness can fill a galaxy with hope."

The other man seemed startled. "Isn't that a Jedi saying?"

Bail smiled. Few, except for a Jedi, would know that. "Safe travels, my friend."

"Safe travels," the man repeated, and walked through the air lock into his ship.

"You didn't tell them my name?" Bail asked C-3PO.

"Of course I didn't, Senator Organa. But this entire ordeal has rather stressed my circuits. Permission to shut down?"

"Granted," Bail said.

C-3PO powered off and slumped. Organa waited until the lights faded from the droid's photoreceptors, then knelt beside R2-D2. "You recorded everything?"

R2-D2 beeped a friendly affirmative.

"Good," Bail said. "Show me what you have on your . . . 'rebels.'"

PART 3
OLD MASTERS

CHAPTER 9

Ezra closed his eyes and tried to forget where he was, what he was doing. That proved difficult when gusts of cold wind from a nearby mountain peak threatened to topple his handstand while his palms had almost frozen to the *Ghost*'s icy hull.

"Focus," Kanan said. "Focus on letting go."

"I'm trying," Ezra said. Unlike the *Ghost*, he couldn't hover at this altitude on repulsors. If he lost his balance and tumbled off the ship, it was a thousand-meter drop to the surface of Lothal below.

"Do or do not," Kanan said. "There is no try."

Ezra opened one eye. "What does that even mean? How can I do something if I don't try to do it?"

Kanan stood on the hull two meters away and pondered his own words. "Actually, that one always confused me, too. But Master Yoda sure used to say it a lot."

Sitting next to Chopper and a bin of empty blue milk containers, Zeb yawned. "C'mon, kid, amuse me. Use the Force!"

Ezra's other eye opened to glare at Zeb— and in that moment of anger, his handstand collapsed and he nearly fell off the ship. Kanan went to him and helped him up.

"There will always be distractions. You need to learn to focus through them. Let's try something else." Kanan clicked together the two pieces of his lightsaber hilt and gave it to Ezra.

Ezra examined the weapon of the Jedi Knights. He loved the feel of it in his hand.

"Having a laser sword doesn't make you

REBEL FIGHTERS

DEFEAT THE EMPIRE

RESTORE THE REPUBLIC

SAVE THE GALAXY

a Jedi," Kanan said, as if he could read Ezra's mind.

"Gets me closer." Ezra activated the blade, then, under Kanan's direction, retracted it to a length that matched his height.

"Close your eyes," Kanan said. "Chopper, let him have it."

Waiting with the lightsaber, Ezra shut his eyes and listened to the whir of the droid's arm as it scooped a small jug out of the bin and pitched it at him. But listening wasn't the same as seeing. Ezra sliced only air while the jug hit him in the side. "Ow!"

He didn't fare any better swinging at the next couple of rocks—and they hurt more.

"That's it, kid! Use your body to slow down that trash," Zeb said. Chopper sniggered and tossed three more rocks. All zipped past Ezra's blade to whack him in various places.

"You're not focusing," Kanan said.

How could Ezra focus when he couldn't look? People focused with their eyes. These blind training techniques were stupid and made him angry.

He lashed out with the blade at the next milk container Chopper threw, determined to cleave it in half. As before, he missed, though this container struck him in the forehead.

His vision returned—now he saw stars. The whole galaxy seemed to whirl around him, and he staggered back, off the side of the *Ghost*.

"Ezra!" Kanan shouted.

Ezra fell, then was jerked back as if his body was tied to an invisible rope. He opened his eyes to see Kanan leaning off the ship, stretching a hand toward him, his face strained.

Ezra was astonished. He could barely levitate a breakfast bowl with the Force. Kanan Jarrus, on the other hand, was using the Force to hold him in place.

Zeb dangled from a hook, grabbed Ezra, and swung back onto the hull. After Ezra gathered his breath, they went inside the ship. That day's lesson was over.

"You're unfocused. You're undisciplined and full of self-doubt," Kanan said.

"And whose fault is that, *Master*?" Ezra asked.

Kanan sighed, as if conceding the point. "It's . . . difficult to teach." He walked down the ship's corridor into the cockpit. Zeb and Chopper squeezed by Ezra to follow.

"He means it's difficult to teach *you*," Zeb said.

Ezra frowned. That wasn't fair. All Kanan did was preach riddles and mantras, without giving specific instruction. He pushed past the Lasat to enter the cockpit. "Kanan . . ."

Sabine shushed him. She, Hera, and Kanan were watching a holonet broadcast on the console. The impeccably dressed Kastle, the anchor of Imperial Holonet News, reported on a stolen TIE fighter that had attacked a transport carrying innocent workers.

The report was a lie. A week earlier, Ezra and Zeb had taken the TIE and used it to free slave laborers on the transport. The mission had brought the two of them closer together briefly, until Zeb returned to his usual thorny self.

"In other news—"

The symbol of the Old Republic broke into the broadcast, and the two-dimensional image of an old man appeared. "Citizens, this is Senator-in-Exile Gall Trayvis. I bring more news that the Empire doesn't want you to hear. One of the Republic's greatest peacekeepers, Jedi Master Luminara Unduli, is alive."

Static-filled footage showed a female in robes. Her large purple headdress revealed only a beautiful face, with royal-blue eyes set against yellow-green skin.

"She has been imprisoned unlawfully, somewhere in the Stygeon system. As citizens, we demand the Emperor produce Master Unduli and grant her a fair trial before the Senate—"

Trayvis said no more as the Imperial emblem replaced his image. Sabine switched off the broadcast. Ezra glanced at Kanan, who still looked at the console, lost in thought.

"This Luminara. You knew her?" Ezra asked.

"I met her once. She was a great Jedi Master—brave, compassionate, disciplined. In fact, she'd make an excellent teacher for you."

A teacher? That wasn't the answer Ezra had expected. Nor was it something he desired. All he wanted from Kanan was better lessons.

Kanan turned to Hera. "There's always been rumors she survived the Clone Wars, but they never came up with a specific location before. We can't pass this up."

Hera started keying the navicomputer. "I'll set course to the Stygeon system."

"The rest of you," Kanan said, "prep for an op."

Everyone went to get ready, leaving Chopper and Ezra in the cockpit. "You hear that?" Ezra said to the droid. "He's going to pawn me off on some stranger."

Chopper rolled away without a beep.

CHAPTER 10

Ezra sat in the rear compartment of the *Ghost*'s auxiliary craft, the *Phantom*, as it detached from its mother ship. In the fold-out seats around him, Zeb checked his bo-rifle, Sabine put on her helmet, and Kanan stared forward at nothing.

"Going in quiet. Hang on," Hera said from the cockpit.

The *Phantom* descended through the turbulent upper atmosphere of Stygeon Prime. Planetary records revealed little about the cloud-covered world, except that semi-intelligent, flat-winged creatures known as tibidees inhabited the skies. On the mountainous surface below lay the Spire, the Imperial detainment facility that held Luminara.

The Spire was supposedly impregnable, protected by blast-proof ray shields, anti-starcraft weaponry, squadrons of TIE fighters, and sensitive long-range scanners that probably would have detected the *Ghost* even with its stealth measures. The team had left Chopper to fly the freighter in orbit while they relied on the *Phantom*'s whisper-mode engines and a special jammer Sabine had rigged to stay concealed from the prison's scanners.

"Thirty seconds," Hera said. "Good luck."

"Luck? We're going to need a miracle," Zeb said.

"Here are three," Sabine said. She handed two thermal detonators to Zeb and one to Ezra.

Ezra turned the detonator over in his hand, careful not to touch the timer button. A thermal had the power to obliterate anything within a small radius.

"Try to stay focused," Kanan said.

Ezra looked at Kanan. "Thought there was no try."

Kanan frowned and looked forward again. Ezra had touched a nerve.

Hera took the *Phantom* on a dive and opened the rear hatch. The Spire's searchlight broke through the clouds but missed finding the ship. All was going according to plan. Kanan took the lead and leapt out toward the prison's sentry platform.

The plan next called for Ezra to ride piggyback on Zeb. But Ezra had made jumps like this before, like when he'd sprung onto the *Ghost*'s ramp with the crate of blasters and when he'd leapt from roof to roof on Garel. If Kanan didn't believe he could make the jump, he'd show the Jedi he could.

"Kid, wait! What're you doing . . . ?" Zeb's words trailed off as Ezra jumped out the hatch.

He soared through the dark clouds and saw Kanan below on the platform, looking up at him. Ezra smiled. Nothing like showing a teacher you were better than he had thought.

Ezra's landing on the platform sure didn't demonstrate that. The impact sent a massive jolt through his body. He staggered into the heavy blast door before collapsing on his rear.

The platform door opened briefly and four

stormtroopers came out, raising their weapons at Ezra. If it hadn't been for the others, he would have been blasted right there.

The *Phantom* whooshed under the platform, and Zeb hopped out, with Sabine on his back. The Lasat grabbed the platform's edge, swung up, and smashed two stormtrooper heads together. Kanan, meanwhile, waved a hand, using the Force to hurtle the two other troopers into the door.

Ezra rose to his feet. "What just happened?" Kanan asked. "You were supposed to exit with Zeb."

Examining the blast door's controls, Sabine interrupted. "Door's locked."

"Got it." Ezra turned to the door, took his astromech arm from his backpack, and began to pick the door lock.

The first adjustments didn't work. Searchlights swept toward them. "Ezra . . ." Kanan said.

"Quiet. I'm focusing."

Click. The blast door opened. Ezra ducked inside the corridor, followed by the others, right as the searchlight passed across the platform.

Kanan strode past Ezra into the corridor. "You're welcome," Ezra said.

Zeb gave Ezra a light smack that stung. "You did your job, kid. Want a medal now?"

Kanan stopped ahead. "Luminara's here. I sense her presence. But it's clouded. . . ."

"First things first," Sabine said. She plugged a decryption device into a security terminal. "I'm borrowing old footage from their datatapes so they'll never know we're here."

The live feed of the corridor shown in the terminal monitor became distorted, then switched to show stormtroopers on guard.

"Nice," Ezra said. As usual, Sabine didn't acknowledge the compliment.

"Where's Luminara?" Kanan asked.

Sabine fiddled with the decryptor and brought up a prison schematic on the monitor.

A cell at the bottom was highlighted.

"Detention block CC01. Isolation cell 0169," she said.

"They have isolation cells on the lower levels? We must've planned off outdated schematics—which means the plan changes." Kanan waved them toward a turbolift bank. "Zeb, Sabine, you're coming along with the kid and me."

"Weren't we supposed to hold our escape route here?"

Kanan pressed the lift button. "The turbolift is now our escape route. Let's go."

The door hissed open and they all entered. Hearing Sabine and Zeb grumble about Kanan's plan, Ezra was glad he wasn't the only one who questioned the Jedi's judgment.

After a short descent, the lift doors opened. Zeb grabbed the two troopers on guard outside, yanked them into the turbolift, and knocked their helmets together. They fell unconscious onto the lift floor.

"Maintain comm silence," Kanan said to Zeb and Sabine. "And whatever you do, hold this lift." He walked out and Ezra followed, according to the plan.

Two more stormtroopers emerged from around the detention block corner. Kanan extended a hand and the troopers collided into the wall. They dropped and remained motionless.

"Wow. You're not messing around tonight," Ezra said.

Kanan ignored the comment, continuing to move down the corridor. Ezra realized he shouldn't have expected a reply. Kanan couldn't wait to ditch him.

A pair of stormtroopers guarded isolation cell 0169. Kanan motioned Ezra to wait in the shadows while he approached, holding up a hand. "Shouldn't you be guarding the Jedi's cell?" Kanan asked. "It's on the next level."

"It's on the next level," one trooper repeated.

"You better get moving," Kanan suggested.

"We better get moving," the second trooper said.

Ezra watched as the troopers hastened away from the cell, down the corridor. Had Kanan just used the Force to influence their minds?

"When do I get to learn that?" Ezra asked. He came forward with his astromech arm to pick the cell door lock.

"Luminara will teach you," Kanan said. He nudged Ezra aside and ignited his lightsaber, then sliced through the door's lock. With a gesture of his hand, he flicked the door open.

Ezra and Kanan entered the narrow cell. At the other end, a stasis field held a female Mirialan in prisoner's fatigues who resembled the Jedi Master in the news report.

"Is it really her?" Ezra asked.

"Yes, but . . ." Kanan hesitated. "Something's wrong."

He walked closer to Luminara and reached a hand into the field. "Master?"

There was a charge of static, the stasis field dissolved, and Luminara disappeared, replaced by a skeleton floating in a sarcophagus. Kanan inhaled in shock. She had been a hologram.

"I don't understand," Ezra said.

"It doesn't seem complicated," said a sinister voice.

Ezra and Kanan whirled. A man all in black entered the cell. His face was as white as a wraith's, offset by glowing yellow eyes. On his bald head and stark cheeks were pointed markings inked in the color of human blood.

He waved his hand as Kanan had done, and the door shut behind him. He pulled a disc off his back, shifted its shape, and ignited one end into a lightsaber.

Unlike Kanan's, his blade was red.

"I am the Inquisitor. Welcome," he said with a smile that wasn't welcoming at all.

CHAPTER **11**

Ezra's anger at Kanan vanished at the sight of the ghoulish man. Now Ezra felt only one emotion—pure, unbridled fear. He sensed the same from Kanan.

The Inquisitor advanced toward them, pointing his lightsaber at the skeleton. "Yes, I'm afraid Master Luminara died with the Republic. And her bones continue to serve the Empire, luring the last Jedi to their ends."

Kanan lunged with his lightsaber, attacking the Inquisitor in a series of practiced moves. The Inquisitor retreated to the door but parried each of the Jedi's swings.

"Interesting," the Inquisitor said. "It seems you trained with Jedi Master Depa Billaba."

"How do you . . ." Kanan's eyes widened. "Who are you?"

Sparks flew off their blades as the Inquisitor drove Kanan back with a flurry of strikes. "The Temple records are quite complete. In close-quarters fighting, Billaba's emphasis was always on form three, which you favor to a ridiculous degree."

The duel shifted toward Ezra, and he dove under their lightsabers and ran toward the door. The Inquisitor pressed forward, kicking Kanan in the chest and sending him backward. Kanan slumped against the rear wall. Luminara's skull seemed to stare at him through the portal window of the sarcophagus.

"Clearly you were a poor student," the Inquisitor said.

Positioned behind the Inquisitor, Ezra fired a stun-ball.

The Inquisitor wheeled, deflecting the

stun-ball with his lightsaber. Ezra backed up and fired again. The Inquisitor didn't block with his lightsaber this time. He allowed the stun-ball to hit him. Energy crackled over his chest armor plate and faded.

"Is that really all you've got, boy?" he asked.

Ezra indicated the thermal detonator he had affixed near the door. "Well, I've got that."

He dropped to the ground. The detonator's timer beeped and it blew.

The explosion tore open the cell door and tossed the Inquisitor into a side wall. Ezra pushed himself up to find Kanan back on his feet.

"Thanks," the Jedi said.

"You're welcome," Ezra said.

They raced out the door into the corridor. They hadn't gone more than a few steps when the Inquisitor appeared behind them.

Ezra reached out with his hand and focused with his mind, urging the Force to thrust the Inquisitor back into the cell.

The Inquisitor swatted off the attack as if it were a gentle breeze. "You have some natural talent, but your training," he said, looking at Kanan, "is almost worse than no training at all."

Kanan turned and charged the Inquisitor. Their lightsabers clashed, over and over in every direction, though the Inquisitor was the better swordsman. He forced Kanan back down the corridor.

"Are you paying attention, boy?" asked the Inquisitor. "The Jedi are dead, but there is another path. The dark side."

"Never heard of it." Ezra pulled back on his slingshot and fired at the Inquisitor's head.

The shot was perfectly aimed and would have downed even Zeb. Yet for the Inquisitor it was nothing. He brought up his blade, deflected the stun-ball, then, with a sweep of his hand, summoned the Force to slam Ezra into the wall.

Ezra fell to his knees. He couldn't move. He

felt like a bantha had stomped on him.

Kanan used the distraction to drive the duel away from Ezra. The Inquisitor chuckled. "Do you really believe you can save the boy? For his sake, surrender."

"I'm not making deals with you," Kanan said.

"Then we'll let him make one," the Inquisitor said. From the other end of his ringed hilt ignited a second red blade that parried Kanan's swing.

Kanan's moment of surprise at seeing the double blades was a moment too long. The Inquisitor extended his arm and had the Force throw Kanan down the hall, far from Ezra.

Ezra wobbled to his feet, raising his slingshot. The Inquisitor strode toward him. "Your 'master' cannot save you, boy. He is unfocused and undisciplined."

"Then we're perfect for each other," Ezra said. Before he got to fire, the Inquisitor flew upward, smashing into the ceiling.

Kanan stood behind him, lowering his arm. Ezra didn't wait for the Inquisitor to fall. He sprinted to his teacher and the two ran down the corridor.

"Guys, this way!" Sabine called out from ahead. They met up with her and Zeb around the corner.

"So you figured out it was a trap," Kanan said. "Our new exit?"

"Landing platform," Sabine said.

All together they dashed toward a set of blast doors. An alarm rang out and red emergency lights blinked. In the middle of the hallway, hidden security doors started to close.

They all leapt through the first door while the Inquisitor chased after them, spinning his dual blades. He extended a hand and the door remained open, allowing him to dive through.

"*Karabast!*" Zeb cursed. "Who's that?"

There was no time for an explanation. The second security door was nearly half closed. Zeb jumped into the gap and held the door,

veins popping from his strained muscles. Kanan, Ezra, and Sabine slipped through; then Zeb dropped down on the other side. The security door shut right before the Inquisitor could make it.

Only one barrier remained before them: the blast doors that went out onto the landing platform. Kanan accessed the control panel. The doors were locked. Sabine applied her decryptor and Ezra his astromech arm, yet the doors still wouldn't open.

Kanan turned off his lightsaber and closed his eyes. "Ezra, together."

"Seriously?" Ezra asked.

"Yes. Picture the locking mechanism in your mind."

The Inquisitor's red saber stabbed through the security door behind them. He would be on them soon.

Kanan raised a hand to the blast doors. Ezra closed his eyes and did the same. Imagining the lock came easy, for he had picked so many on Lothal. Now he became his astromech arm, adjusting himself for the lock's pathways. He wasn't alone, either: he felt the Jedi's presence with him, giving him strength and prodding him along, like an encouraging teacher.

The door opened as Ezra opened his eyes. Stormtroopers and TIE fighter pilots could be glimpsed behind it.

"One last miracle," Zeb said, and threw his detonator through the door. Troopers and pilots went up in a boom.

The four ran out through the smoke to duck behind crates on the platform. While the others blasted at the Imperials, Sabine contacted the *Phantom* for a pickup.

"On my way, Spectre-5. And I'm bringing the fleet," Hera commed back.

"We have a fleet?" Zeb asked.

"We do now," Hera responded.

The *Phantom* swooped down, and with it came a flock of tibidees, the broad-winged creatures that resembled kites. Their numbers made it impossible for the Spire's cannons to target the ship. In the ensuing chaos, Ezra and the others ran toward the descending *Phantom*.

Not every enemy was distracted. A double-bladed lightsaber whirled through the air toward them—only to be deflected at the last moment by Kanan.

The lightsaber spun back, caught by the Inquisitor near the blast doors.

"Does yours do that?" Zeb asked.

Kanan pushed Zeb and the others into the *Phantom* before the Inquisitor could strike again. As the hatch closed, Ezra saw the Inquisitor's yellow eyes burning with hate.

CHAPTER 12

Ezra leaned against the *Ghost*'s
common room wall. The crew had landed on
the plains of Lothal, where, unlike Stygeon
Prime, the air was fresh and the sun shone.
Despite that, all anyone wanted to do was
watch the holonet.

"We regret to report that Luminara Unduli
has been eliminated by rebel extremists,"
announced Imperial Holonet News anchor
Kastle.

Ezra felt anger boil off Kanan in waves.
Kastle continued. "The Jedi Master was en
route to offer testimony before the Imperial
Senate—"

The signal rippled, and a new figure cut into the broadcast. "Citizens, this is Senator-in-Exile Gall Trayvis, advising you not to take the Empire's version of these events at face value. More importantly, I urge you to keep Master Luminara's memory alive."

Ezra had no use for news he already knew. He left the common room, hearing Zeb behind him. "Least we made sure no other Jedi fell into the Inquisitor's trap. That's something, right?"

Something indeed. There could be more Jedi to fight foes like the Inquisitor if Kanan wanted to teach. But the man hadn't said anything to Ezra since Stygeon. It was as if they hadn't cooperated at all.

He walked out of the ship and sat cross-legged in the soft grass. It rustled around him, soothing him, giving him peace he hadn't had in days.

Grass crunched behind him. Ezra didn't need to turn to know who it was. "Look, I know

you wanted to dump me on Luminara," he said. "Just because she's gone, it doesn't mean you're stuck with me."

Kanan sat down beside him. "I don't want to dump you. I just wanted you to have the best teacher."

"Well, I don't want the best teacher—I want you!" The words slipped out of Ezra's mouth before he realized what he was saying. "Not that you're not the best, I—"

"Ezra, I'm not going to try to teach you anymore," Kanan said.

Ezra looked away in disappointment. This Jedi was nothing but a fake.

Kanan wasn't done. "If all I do is try, that means I don't truly believe I can succeed. So from now on, I *will* teach you."

Kanan placed a hand on Ezra's shoulder. "I may fail. You may fail. But there is no try."

Ezra looked up. Kanan wasn't a fake. He was just cautious, as Ezra was. Those dark times demanded one to be.

"I . . . understand, Master," Ezra said.

"Let's see if you do."

Kanan tossed Ezra his lightsaber. Ezra caught it and thumbed the activation switch. The blue blade hummed to life. Ezra adjusted its length and closed his eyes, and Kanan began to pitch rocks.

ABOUT THE AUTHOR

MICHAEL KOGGE has written in the *Star Wars* galaxy for a long, long time. His other recent work includes *Empire of the Wolf,* an epic comic series featuring werewolves in ancient Rome, published by Alterna Comics. He lives online at www.michaelkogge.com, while his real home is located in Los Angeles.